For our Alan, with love

Sue Hendra & Paul Linnet

ALADDIN

New York · London
Toronto · Sydney · New Delhi

Alan the bear loved whizzing down the very tall slide with his friends.

WAHOOO! WHEEEEE!

It was SO MUCH FUN!

"Let's go on again!" said Alan.

"Alan, why are you dancing?"
asked Giraffe.

"I'm not dancing!" said Alan. "I need to wee!
But first I need just one more go."

"No," said Giraffe. "When you've got to go,
you've got to go."

But getting Alan to the bathroom
wasn't going to be easy.

"Ooooh, just one balloon!"
he cried.

"Alan, come on, before it's too late,"
said Giraffe.

Then Alan saw Claude's party.

"Ooooh, just one piece of cake!"
Alan cried.

"No time!" said Robot.

Finally they got there.

"Oh dear," said Giraffe. "Can you hold on?
It's going to be a long wait."

"But I can't wait," said Alan.

"Don't worry!" called a little dolly.
"I can help. You can come to my house!"

"PHEW!" said the friends.

"Oh no! I can't wee in there," said Alan.
"It's a teeny tiny toilet!"

And off he went.

"No! You can't wee in there!" yelled Robot.
"It's a teapot—not a wee-pot!"

"How about this hat?" said Alan. "It's perfect."

And he was just about to wee when . . .

"Don't even think about it!"
said Magic Rabbit.

"Yikes! Sorry," said Alan,
dancing about again. "It's just . . ."

By now things were getting desperate.

"Quick, behind that curtain!" shouted Robot.

But when Alan turned around, he realized he was dancing furiously in front of a huge audience!

The crowd whooped. They cheered.
They'd never seen dancing like it!

"And the winner of the International Toy Dancing Competition is . . ."

"Alan. My name's Alan."

"And how do you feel to have won the cup, Alan?"

"Ahhhhh!" said Alan at last.
"I feel fantastic!"

"Well, what a relief," said Robot, smiling. "Thank goodness you don't need to wee anymore."

"Oh no, I definitely do!" Alan grinned.

ALADDIN
An imprint of Simon & Schuster Children's Publishing Division
1230 Avenue of the Americas, New York, New York 10020
This Aladdin hardcover edition July 2019
Copyright © 2015 by Sue Hendra and Paul Linnet
Published by arrangement with Simon & Schuster UK Ltd.
Originally published in Great Britain in 2015
All rights reserved, including the right of reproduction in whole or in part in any form.
ALADDIN and related logo are registered trademarks of Simon & Schuster, Inc.
For information about special discounts for bulk purchases,
please contact Simon & Schuster Special Sales at 1-866-506-1949
or business@simonandschuster.com.
The Simon & Schuster Speakers Bureau can bring authors to your live event.
For more information or to book an event contact the Simon & Schuster Speakers Bureau
at 1-866-248-3049 or visit our website at www.simonspeakers.com.
The text of this book was set in Happyjamas.
Manufactured in China 0419 SCP
2 4 6 8 10 9 7 5 3 1
Library of Congress Control Number 2018944312
ISBN 978-1-4814-9039-9 (hc)
ISBN 978-1-4814-9040-5 (eBook)

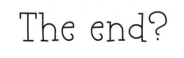

The end?

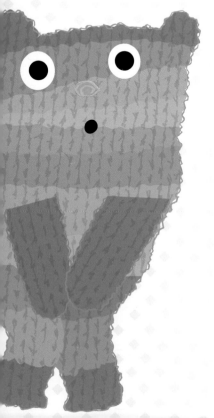